# When Addie Was Scared

*This book is for our father, Harry, and our mother, the Addie in this story — L.B.*
*For my daughters Loren and Liza, for Ken, and for Addie — W.B.*

Kids Can Press acknowledges the financial support of the Ontario Arts Council, the Canada Council for the Arts and the Department of Cultural Heritage.

Published in Canada by
Kids Can Press Ltd.
29 Birch Avenue
Toronto, ON  M4V 1E2

Published in the U.S. by
Kids Can Press Ltd.
85 River Rock Drive, Suite 202
Buffalo, NY  14207

The artwork in this book was rendered in watercolor.
Text is set in Albertus.

Edited by Debbie Rogosin
Designed by Marie Bartholomew

Printed and bound in Hong Kong, China, by Book Art Inc., Toronto

CM 99 0 9 8 7 6 5 4 3 2 1

**Canadian Cataloguing in Publication Data**

Bailey, Linda, 1948 —
    When Addie was scared

ISBN 1-55074-431-3

I. Bailey, Wendy. II. Title.

PS8553.A3644W43      1999     jC813'.54      C99-930240-X
PZ7.B34Wh   1999

Kids Can Press is a Nelvana company.

# When Addie Was Scared

## Linda Bailey • Wendy Bailey

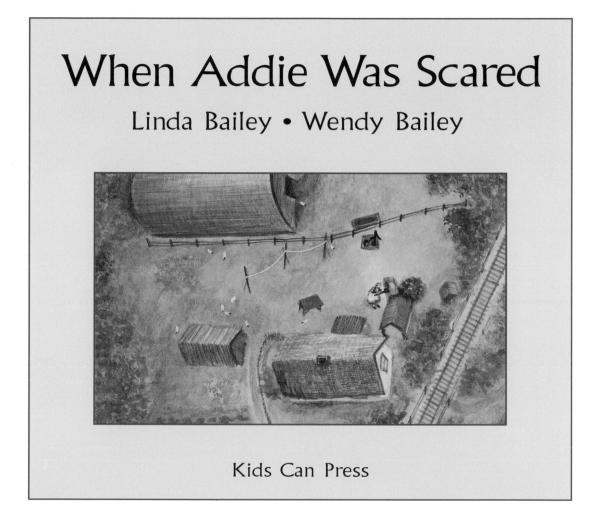

Kids Can Press

Addie was scared of almost everything.
There were plenty of things to be scared of,
out there in the bush where she lived.

She was scared of the big turkey gobbler in the yard. It chased her onto a buggy once and kept her there all afternoon.

After that, Addie gave the gobbler all the room it needed to be mean.

She was scared of the wild things that lived in the bush. When Addie went to get the cows in the evening, she sang. She sang in her loudest voice so she wouldn't have to listen to the chitters and crackles and creaks of things she couldn't see.

She sang so loud that neighbors half a mile away could hear her. "Oh, that Addie," they said, "she sure loves to sing."

She was scared of wolves, even though she'd never seen one. At night, in the winter, Addie lay in bed and listened to their long, cold cries—now farther, now closer.

She lay between her sisters, her heart beating hard, scared of the long, cold walk to school the next day.

Scared of seeing tracks in the snow.

Addie was scared of bulls too. There was a big one on the way to Babcha's house. Babcha was Addie's granny, and she was old, and Addie loved her more than anything. Addie walked to Babcha's house every Saturday to wash the floor and help her feed the chickens.

The bull didn't stop Addie from visiting Babcha. But it did make her walk a whole extra mile to get there.

Thunderstorms. Oh, they were scary. One day Addie was taking a basket of eggs home from Babcha's house when black clouds rolled across the sky. Lightning blazed and thunder crashed — so wild, so bright, so loud, it was like the whole sky was ripping apart.

Addie's breath stopped. Her heart froze. She threw those eggs as hard as she could into the bush and ran, ran, ran. She ran the whole mile back and was soaked with sweat when finally she leaped into Babcha's arms.

Babcha's arms were warm. Her hands were strong. Her lap was safe. She held Addie tight in the doorway.

Together they watched as the storm tore the sky wide open.

Sometimes Addie was scared of things that weren't even there.

She stayed home one day while the others went to pick berries. When she heard a scritch-scritch, she thought—rat! She jumped onto the kitchen table and crouched there, trembling.

She was still there when the others came home.

And that's how it was for Addie. Scared. Until one afternoon at Babcha's house.

Addie was hanging laundry on the line. Babcha was in the barn. The chickens were pecking in the yard. Everything quiet, and then—

A flutter. A squawk.
A sudden loud screech!
The chickens were
running. What? Where?
Addie looked up.
Curved claws,
thundering wings,
something terrible
out of the sky—

Chicken hawk! Come
to steal Babcha's
chickens! Addie let out
a tiny scream. She
started to run away.
The chickens scurried
around her feet. The
hawk circled. It
swooped.

That's when, inside
Addie, something
caught. Something
deep, something brave,
something angry, and—

Addie turned. She screamed again. This time she screamed—loud and wild and fierce—right at the hawk.

"NO!"

She looked around. Grabbing a branch, she began to flail it as hard as she could at the sky.

"No!" she shrieked. "No!"

Babcha came running from the barn. She grabbed a branch to help. Addie and Babcha ran among the chickens, yelling and beating at the sky.

The hawk flew away.

Babcha hugged Addie hard. She told Addie what a big, brave girl she was. She cut thick slices of bread and brought out cranberry jam. Addie and Babcha sat and ate together in the sunshine of the yard.

This was not the end of being scared for Addie. Oh, no. She still jumped every time she heard a crackle in the bush. She still walked an extra mile to get around the bull. But these were small things.

What mattered was this. Addie had found a place inside herself where she was as strong as any bull and as fierce as any hawk.

When she needed it, it would be there.